Rainbow
Seeker

Lee D. Gee, M.S.Ed

Nicco:
I wrote this for you
and your enjoyment.
Uncle Lee

AuthorHouse™
1663 Liberty Drive
Bloomington, IN 47403
www.authorhouse.com
Phone: 1-800-839-8640

Rainbow Seeker *is a testimony to Kim's character and personality and who he is, rather than to what he does; it's also a work of fiction. Names, characters, places, and incidents are the product of the author's imagination or are used fictitiously. Resemblance to actual events, locales, or persons, living or dead, is taken from various experiences in the author's life.*

First published by AuthorHouse 11/17/2011

ISBN: 978-1-4670-3859-1 (sc)

Printed in the United States of America

Any people depicted in stock imagery provided by Thinkstock are models,
and such images are being used for illustrative purposes only.
Certain stock imagery © Thinkstock.

This book is printed on acid-free paper.

Because of the dynamic nature of the Internet, any web addresses or links contained in this book may have changed since publication and may no longer be valid. The views expressed in this work are solely those of the author and do not necessarily reflect the views of the publisher, and the publisher hereby disclaims any responsibility for them.

authorHOUSE®

In memory
of
Glenna Virginia Gee

Rainbow Seeker is a collection of short stories about different periods in the life of a teenager. Kim is an Asian American teenager, but his clashes are no different than those of any teenager. Each story depicts particular times, characteristics and virtues most teenagers, and young men and women, experience as they mature. For example, the theme in *Discovery* deals with the struggle of self identity and loneliness many teenagers confront, which drives them to seek a place in the group; in other words, wanting to fit in. *The Cruise* illustrates empathy, sympathy, and courage in challenging times. And, there seems to be at least one family outing that will always stay with us. *The Black Out* is just such a family outing. It demonstrates family adventure, as well as aiding a neighbor in distress. Being a part of something larger than one-self, especially family roots, is the bases for *Lost Peony*. Finally, everyone loves a happy ending. And, even though it too was a struggle, Kim finds love.

Once a job has begun,
Never leave it until it's done.
Be the labor great or small,
Do it well,
Or not at all.

—Ms. Clark, 3rd grade teacher

"A belief is not an idea that the mind possess;
it is an idea that possess the mind."

—Anonymous

"Things that you do for yourself go to the grave with you;
but, things you do for someone else
can live on indefinitely"

—Anonymous

Be Bio-Hermeneutic,
It's rewarding.

—Lee D. Gee

.. A NOTE TO THE READER ..

I have always had a vivid imagination, but my ability to put on paper and capture the visions in my mind wasn't possible until I took an English course in summer school in 1962. I only took the course to graduate from high school a year early. Nevertheless, I learned more during that six week course than I had in all of the previous English courses. I only hope that the stories that follow demonstrate my English comprehension.

Writing short stories was inspired by my grandson, DJ, when he gave me a copy of a story he wrote in middle school. I wrote my first story as a gift to DJ with hopes of developing a bond between us. You see, I knew of DJ but he lived in Orlando, Florida.

In the series that follow, I have incorporated a little of my life experiences. For example, *Discoveries* address feelings of isolation and loneliness I harbored throughout my elementary and high school years. Thus, graduating from high school and joining the military was my way of starting my life over and being the person I wanted to be, rather than the person I thought I needed to be to survive. Economically, college was not an option. In *The Cruise*, it captures my penchant to help others. I have never been a selfish person or one to ignore doing the right thing. So, combining these feelings with my colorful imagination is captured in that particular story. On the other hand, *The Black-out*, is in part a true story of a short excursion the family and visiting in-laws took to New York City. In short, our best laid plans went astray due to "the black-out." *Lost Peony* and *Lucky* captures my adventurous as well as my romantic side. When I took a three month sabbatical from Community College of Allegheny County and went to China for the first time, it was not only fulfilling one of my two greatest dreams, i.e., going to China, but it was also a real exploration and voyage. *Lucky* depicts a collection of escapades on different and subsequent trips. The title is the translation of my Chinese name, *Gee Lee*.

These stories were initially written to amuse and indulge myself. But, after I had written a few, I realized I wanted to write for young people, most specifically, my grandchildren. I hope all that reads these stories will find as much enjoyment in them as I did during their creation.

Yee Kim Poy was my father's Chinese name; he was from Guangzhou (aka Canton), Guangdong Province.

The adventure isn't over.

CONTENTS

DISCOVERIES

"Xiao Tu! … Xiao Tu! …Chi fan! Kuai! Kuai!" His mother calls him to hurry for dinner. She calls him little rabbit because he was born in the year of the rabbit. His Chinese name is Yee Kim Poy, although he's known in school as Kim Yee.

Kim is a 15-year-old American-Chinese boy living in small town U.S.A. He is known as Kim Yee because in America the family name comes last, rather than first as in China. His family is the only Chinese family in the community; and, he – of course – is the only Asian in his school. Kim is a very likable young boy, friendly, extremely intelligent, and very mature for his age. He loves music and sports, and participates in the school band as a saxophone player and is a member of the track team. He runs the low hurdles.

On the surface, one would think that Kim's life is as normal as most in small town U. S. A., and that Kim is a well-adjusted and amiable kid. But the fact is, Kim is very unhappy and worried.

Kim's physical characteristics, his Asian look, and intelligence, being in the top 1% of his class, festers feelings of isolation, loneliness, and "oneness." Without a doubt, he stands out in a crowd. Everyone in the school knows of him, and/or knows his name, but Kim has a very small circle of friends, even though he knows most of his classmates by name.

Ordinarily, after school each day and week-ends, Kim plays a lot of sand lot sports with the kids in the neighborhood; but, because he is so self disciplined, he interrupts the games to go home to complete his studies before bed, often times eating dinner late.

Because of Kim's competitive nature, he excels in academics to prove to himself that he's as good – if not better – than most of his European classmates. As a result of his self-imposed academic challenges, Kim entered a national science contest and his project won first place. The school principal, counselor, science teachers, and student body were all surprised to learn of Kim's success. They all discovered Kim's national recognition when the local paper published an article about his accomplishment. Of course, this lead to more recognition and celebrations, all of which Kim desperately tried to avoid. Luckily for Kim, all of these celebrations and awards ceremonies came at the end of the school year.

For Kim, he wanted to spend his summer in anonymity, but all of this attention put a spotlight on a person who already felt the subtle glares of his community. For these reasons, Kim "escaped" in the middle of the night and journeyed off to the big city. There he felt he could lose himself in the crowd, be himself and regain his anonymity.

The excitement of arriving in the city was so awe-inspiring that Kim paid very little attention to the fact that he was homeless, jobless, and penniless. The "rush" he felt, from the hundreds of people hurrying off to their individual destinies, whizzing past him as if he were an obstacle in their path, was the closest sense of absolute freedom he had ever felt. Kim was amazed and delighted with his new found liberty.

But just as quickly as he tasted the sweetness of liberty, he woke up to the reality of homelessness. Kim knew he had to find work quickly.

Lucky for Kim, he found his way to the multicultural garment district of the city. There, cheap labor, few questions, and questionable documentation were the norm for employment. Thus, Kim found work in a small factory, populated mostly by females, and located near a struggling elementary school. As a "utility" man, Kim moved freely about the factory, picking up requests and delivering supplies. On occasions, he filled-in as the "sanitation engineer." The job did not pay much, but it helped meet his basic need, and he was happy.

After a week or so on the job, Kim got noticed by three young ladies – each a friend of the other – and each working in a different department. All three young ladies are extremely beautiful, pleasant, friendly and smart. The white girl (Katie) had a "jerk" for a boyfriend. Kim was in infatuated with her. But, she was in love with the jerk. The black female, Shayna, and Kim are probably the closest, in terms of friendship and appreciation for each other. Their friendship may be the strongest of the three. Shayna has a boyfriend (Marc) who completes a very strong triad between the three. Finally, there's Tsu, the Chinese female. She's in love with Kim, but he's too thick headed to recognize it. Although, they get along great. In fact, from time to time, if all six didn't get together for lunch, then the four employees definitely would.

It was at one of these various lunch meetings that Kim discovered the small factory was in trouble, and everyone was worried about losing their jobs. "What are we going to do if the factory closes?" Katie asked her girl friends. "I don't know," was Shayna's response. "I'll probably have to work for my uncle in his laundry," Tsu said, dreading the idea. Thus, lay-offs and closings dominated their lunch discussions. And, therein was the problem for Kim. That is, he could reveal his upper-middle class identity and his potent intellect by suggesting ideas, but would lose the respect of his friends; or, do nothing and allow fate to take its course and see his friends suffer the pain of unemployment and the emotional distress that accompanied uncertainty.

On the job, Kim presented himself as a quiet, shy and somewhat nerdy boy. He very seldom talked to anyone about his ideas and etc. So, on occasions, to maintain his anonymity, Kim would ride the local tourist train and sit just behind the engineer. With the noise of the engine and the sounds of the wheels on the tracks, Kim was able to carry on one-sided conversations with the engineer and hear his thoughts aloud with confidence. He talked about his feelings, his family, his concerns about the future, his job, his co-workers, and more.

It was on one of these train rides that Kim plotted and planned strategies to help the factory. Using the factory's "Employee Suggestion Box," Kim – secretly – dropped in his suggestions that quickly became adopted by the owner. And, of course, the lunch time conversations, as well as throughout the factory, now focused on the mystery person who offers the suggestions but accepted no recognition or reward.

Kim understood the "suggestions" were only a band-aid approach to a larger problem; and, unless a real solution was found, the factory would close.

Making a bold and daring decision, Kim puts his entire future on the line. The decision will not only risk his true identity, but also his freedom.

Knowing how city bureaucracy operates, Kim knew that any changes in city plans would not be discovered until it was too late. Therefore, he broke into the office of the City Planner and made a "few" changes to plans that would have meant taking the factory property, under the authority of eminent domain, for the use of the elementary school. Kim's changes were a win-win-win for everyone; that is, the school, the factory, and the city's budget.

Even though the "new" project was well on its way, only one problem remained. The Chief of the planning department discovered the changes too late, as Kim expected, and he wanted "justice." The Chief also found the Asian lucky charm Kim's grandfather had given him. The lucky charm was lost in the Chief's office the night Kim broke in. The Chief knew who ever owned the lucky charm was the burglar.

Fate has a way of showing its ugly face at the wrong time. One day, after a very hard and long rain, a delivery truck got stuck in a mud hole at the school's construction site. In all the panic to free the truck, some old newspapers – the truck was taking to the city's re-cycling center – had to be taken from the truck to lighten its load.

A small bundle of these old newspapers ended up in the doorway of the small factory. And, Katie's boyfriend, who also happens to be an enthusiast for the "funnies," was rumbling through the papers as he waited on Katie. There he discovered a picture of Kim, his missing person announcement, and information about his accomplishments. Because the picture was faded, due to water damage, Kim's identity was uncertain; but, the picture also exposed the lucky charm Kim wore so proudly.

The jerk, with the intention of embarrassing and humiliating Kim, secretly spread the knowledge of Kim's identity. What the jerk didn't know – of course – was that Kim lost his lucky charm in the office of the city planner.

The Director of City Planning also has a son that attends the same art school of Shayna's boyfriend - Marc. So, during family dinner, when the director's son was relating the story of Kim's identity being discovered and how the lucky charm was the key to the exposure, his father took notice.

This lead to questions from the father; "Who is the Kim that you're talking about?" The Director asked harshly. Stunned at the manner of his father's question, "He's a new kid in town; he's Chinese," was all that he could think of in reply. The Director later researched a copy of the old newspaper article from the city's archives. After comparing the charm in the picture with the one found in his office, he called the police.

In the meantime, Kim was struggling with mending his relationships with the young ladies. Of course, when they learned of Kim's real identity, they felt used and betrayed. "How could you lie like that?" Katie asked angrily. "I ... I ..." was all Kim could get out before Shayna interrupted with, "So, you're a geek with money?" Tsu said nothing. She just looked on in astonishment.

Nevertheless, as a result of Kim's actions, several things happened: Katie and the jerk broke off their relationship because she finally realized he was not the man she thought he was.

Shayna and her boyfriend rallied the community to come to the aid of Kim because the "illegal" changes did in fact save their jobs, caused improvements to the school, increased community pride, and provided hope for the community, as well as save the city money.

Tsu, with Shayna and Marc's help, not only gathered enough support to keep Kim out of jail, but, also opened Kim's eyes to the affection Tsu had for him.

In spite of these positive outcomes, none were more important than the discovery resulting from Kim's journey for belongingness and self-identity. That is to say, Kim's biggest revelation was his realization that he already had membership in a group that is highly respected, has historic lineage, and characterized by its industriousness, i.e., his family and his culture. He did not need to run away from home to learn this, but rather run to the closest mirror.

THE CRUISE

"Wow! I really needed this. I can't believe I'm here. This really feels good," Kim thought to himself as he laid in the hot sun, enjoying the breeze of the ocean, the laughter of kids in the pool, the beat of the calypso music, and the soothing rock of the ship.

Because he was born in the year of the rabbit, his family calls him *Xiao Tu,* little rabbit. But in school and in the Chinese neighborhood, everyone knows him as Yee Kim Poy, or Kim. Like the traits of the rabbit, Kim is talented, affectionate and seeks tranquility. In fact, because he won several contests, he now relaxes quietly on the deck of the Royal Caribbean with his family. The first contest Kim won was a science project where he gained national recognition. In the other competition, he became the state champion in *Qi Gong,* a martial art that is more than 1800 years old. As a result of his recent accomplishments, the family decided to take a long weekend Thanksgiving cruise to the Caribbean Islands as a reward to Kim for his hard work, academic studies and sacrifice.

After a couple of days at sea, the ship was stopping in the Bahamas for a 24-hour shopping and entertainment spree. However, before leaving the ship, the ship's entertainment coordinator provided information and warnings on the best places to shop for great bargains and discounts; "Oh! Before I forget, I remind you to pay close attention to your environment and people around you." she cautioned the passengers, reminding them about the young teen gangs who sailed the streets preying on tourists.

These young hooligans specialized in picking tourists' pockets, snatching women's purses and running into the back allies and wooded areas. Of course, *Xiao Tu's* parents, upon hearing these warnings, took extra precautions to protect their valuables. His *muqin*, mother, shortens the strap of her purse so as to carry it closer to her body and higher under her arm. His *fuqin,* father, checked to make sure his pockets were without holes and his wallet was at the very bottom of his pocket. For Kim's father, it wasn't that he was concerned about his money because he always carried very little, but rather the wallet itself; it was a gift from Kim's grandfather who continues to live on mainland China, and the wallet had the family's seal engraved into the leather.

Needless to say, it was obvious that everyone was excited when the ship finally docked at port because the crowd of people hurried to disembark and participate in the much talked about tradition of bargaining with the local merchants. Later that evening, many of the tourists would compare purchase prices not only to determine who got the best bargain, but to determine who may have been the best negotiator.

"Don't forget Xiao Tu, we will meet at 6." His mother insists on calling him little rabbit even though he's embarrassed by the term. Nonetheless, Kim and his parents had a plan. His parents would journey off in one direction looking for their treasure and Kim would venture off in the opposite direction. However, they did agree to meet at 6:00pm in the town's center to have dinner together. So, Kim had about 5 hours to explore the area alone.

Kim's parents had not been gone for more than an hour when his father discovered his wallet missing. Upset and frustrated, they tried to retrace their steps in hopes they could find the wallet; but, the crowed streets and crowed shops left little hope that the wallet would be found. There was nothing else to do but to make a report of the missing wallet with the police. Thus, off to the police station they went.

As for Kim, he darted in and out of so many shops looking and pricing various items that he didn't realize 2-1/2 hours had passed. When he finally decided to check his watch for the time, he not only realized he only had about one hour to meet his parents for dinner, but he also discovered he had traveled to the end of the "shopping strip" district.

The shoppers were fewer, the storefronts were less decorated, and the distance to the center of town was more than a mile away. Even so, there was nothing to worry about; he had plenty of time remaining before dinner.

Just as Kim turned to head back toward the ship, his parents and restaurants, "Souvenirs?" he was approached by a small almond faced girl, asking him to buy one of her home made souvenirs. "Oh! Maybe," was his response as he turned to examine the trophies. Slowly approaching Kim and the girl was the girl's brother. He was about Kim's age. He moved slowly because he suffered from muscular dystrophy and one leg was shorter than the other.

The affectionate Kim took one look at the brother and sister and immediately started searching through their souvenirs trying to find one he could give to someone as a gift. And as he rambled through the offerings, he and the brother, Alonzo, began talking and sharing information about their favorite sports heroes. "I think Tiger's personal problems have had a major impact on his game," Alonzo presented. "I tend to agree; I just hope it doesn't take too long for him to get back on track, otherwise he'll be yesterday's news," Kim offered. These comparisons and discussions about Michael Jordan, Tiger Woods and Michael Chan naturally lead into other areas of interest. For Kim, it was his curiosity about Alonzo's disability, i.e., how, when and where did the challenge occur? For Alonzo, he seemed more curious and fascinated about Kim's country and life style. Before either boy knew it, almost an hour had passed.

Not only had the two boys neglected the time, they also failed to notice a small band of local teenagers approaching them.

As Kim was about to retrieve his money from his backpack, the leader of the gang stepped between

Kim and Alonzo. With his back to Kim, the gang leader insisted Alonzo gave up all his money. "You know the drill; give it up." Obviously, this has happened before.

At the same time, another gang member was attempting to take the souvenirs from Alonzo's little sister. "Get your hands off of me; leave us alone!" were her shouts as she struggled against all odds. It was at this point that Kim made his presence known. He immediately intervened by trying to stop a bully from taking advantage of a young girl and her helpless brother. "I think you guys are way out of line." Was Kim's warning. By taking this action, Kim drew the attention of the entire gang on himself. The four local ruffians surrounded Kim and their leader took charge. "You have 60 seconds to empty your pockets, or eat knuckles." He yelled, trying to look and act like a drill sergeant, standing within inches of Kim's face.

As a rule, Kim tries to avoid any disturbance that interferes with his tranquil nature. But in this case, avoidance was not possible. The gang members closed their circle around Kim tighter, attempting to prevent him from escaping.

Needless to say, Kim never thought his acts of humanity would lead him into a position of being pushed, threaten, beaten or robbed.

Unknowingly and unfortunately for the gang leader and his small band of tough guys, Kim is the state champion in *Iron Shirt Qi Gong*. Thus, before anyone knew or realized it, each of the gang members found themselves dazed, bewildered and suffering from calculated and strategic blows. Kim had dealt each a swift strike with such lighting speed that they never saw the hit coming.

Of course, the commotion attracted the attention of the local police who were touring the streets looking for the thugs. Two officers quickly arrived at the scene, but the disturbance was over and the serenity of Kim and Alonzo's conversation had returned. However, the gang members laid about the street corner.

Alonzo, without hesitation, explained to the police officers what had happened, and how Kim had defended him and his little sister. With no further explanation necessary, the police officers knew they had captured the teenage gang that was preying on the tourists. The police quickly inspected the bags and pockets of the gang members.

Kim recognized his family's seal on one of the wallets as the police were pulling out wallets, jewelry and rolls of dollar bills.

A closer inspection left no doubt; it was Kim's father's wallet. The police could not release the wallet to Kim; he would have to follow them to the police station, find out if Kim's father filled a stolen wallet report, and then call his parents to come to the police station to retrieve it.

But none of this was necessary; because as Kim, the police and the gang members entered the police station, Kim's parents were coming out of the station's door.

After the wallet was returned to Kim's father, the family had an enjoyable meal at 6:00 PM, just as they had planned.

The Black Out

For Kim, It seemed as though June 23rd would never come. But now that it had finally arrived, 6 O'clock could not come fast enough. Because at 6 O'clock, Kim and his parents were going to the airport to meet the 7:30PM plane from Beijing. Kim's grandparents, *Lao Lao* (grandmother) and *Lao Yie* (grandfather), were finally coming to the USA for the first time. Everyone was excited. You could hear the urgency in Kim's voice, "Mom! Dad! Hurry up we can't be late." It would take a bolt of lighting to strike in order for Kim's father to move faster than the growth of grass, "Hold your horses; we have plenty time."

Kim and his parents, especially Kim's mother who has not seen her parents in more than 5 years, had planned and prepared for the grandparents' vacation for more than a year. Not only would Kim's grandparents have an exciting vacation, but also for Kim his summer promised to be filled with dinners, sightseeing, tours, weekend excursions, and various celebrations. Some of the trips the family had planned included: New York City, Toronto Canada, Washington D.C., and Niagara Falls. For the local sights, the Zoo, Science Center, Conservatory, Museum, Music Hall and Sports Arena were all on the "to do list." Needless to say, lots of pictures would be taken.

But for today, it was off to the airport.

Even though the trip to the airport would take about 30 minutes, everyone decided to leave the house at 6 O'clock just in case there were unexpected traffic jams; and, besides, everyone wanted to be at the gate when Lao Lao and Lao Yie came through the fuselage tunnel into the terminal.

"Mom, Dad, come on!" Kim's voice could hardly be heard as he dashed into the air port. This was after the family found a parking spot. Kim wanted to be the first to enter the terminal, locate the flight monitors to determine which gate the plane from Beijing would dock, and know if the plane from China would arrive on time.

The airport is an exciting place. Traveling through the crowds to the arrival gate, Kim was able to peer between the travelers and through the hugh windows to see some airplanes taking off, some taxing into the gates, trains of mini buses carrying luggage to and from various destinations, and members of the ground crew directing planes into their docking stations. For Kim, the great thing about arriving early at the airport is feeling the excitement and being a part of the busy atmosphere. The worst thing about arriving early is the wait; the wait made him realized how slowly the clock moves toward an arrival time. Still, the plane did arrive on time; Kim's grandparents were excited to see everyone again, and the trip to Kim's house was full of family up-date stories, laughter, and questions about American billboards, signs, buildings, cars, weather, houses and people. "Dajie (older sister) has a new car; DiDi (little brother) received a full scholarship to medical school in Guangzhou; what in the heck does that sign mean? Does everyone on Golden Mountain (United States) live like that?"

Shortly after entering the house, unpacking and putting away the luggage, everyone began washing for dinner. This would be the first time the family would have dinner together in more than 5 years. Kim's mother had prepared a few traditional Chinese dishes: *Bai Chi* (cabbage), *Toufu* (bean curd), *Jiao Zi* (dumplings), *Ji Di* (diced chicken), *Huang Gua* (cucumber), and of course, *Cha* (tea). It was a late dinner, but no one seemed to notice or care. In fact, by the time the kitchen was cleaned, a few more short episodes about family history were told, and Kim's grandparents prepared for their showers, it was close to midnight.

"Xiao Tu, are you going to join us today?" Lao Lao asked. During the first week of his grandparent's vacation, Kim discovered his grandparents always started their day the same. After breakfast, Lao Lao and Lao Yie would walk to the nearby park. Lao Yie would go for his morning walk around the lake, and Lao Lao would perform her morning Tai Chi. After dinner, each day, both Lao Lao and Lao Yie would walk around the lake; and, after supper, everyone would walk around the lake. This routine went on for the entire time Kim's grandparents were in America. "Maybe tomorrow," was always Kim's response. Secretly, he was hoping they would stop asking.

By the middle of the second week, the family was busy preparing for their first trip together. They were all going to take a 7 O'clock train to New York City. The ride would take about 12 hours; therefore, Kim's mother and grandmother made sure enough food would be packed to eat on the train. They had decided to eat at a local restaurant once they were in New York. This would also give them an opportunity to see the local sights as they explored for a good restaurant.

"How much extra did you have to pay for these seats?" Lao Lao asked. Kim's grandparents were surprised at the big difference between the Am-Track train to New York and the trains in China. "No extra charge, Mom. All seats are the same cost." On the American train, everyone got a *soft seat,* and the seats could be turned around to face each other, as well as adjusted enough to allow passengers to sleep comfortably. This was not possible on China's trains, and *soft seats* cost more. The American train was not as crowded and it was air-conditioned. However, they did point out that trains in China moved a lot faster and had fewer stops.

Disembarking the train at Pennsylvania Station in the heart of New York City is similar to many train stations in China. There are announcements over the loud speakers, the sounds of trains braking, the noise from the crowds of people, squeaking luggage wheels, and people rushing about the rotunda. All of these sights and sounds were very familiar to Kim's grandparents. Even when the family surfaced upstairs to the crowded streets above the train station, the sounds of car horns, whistles blowing, people' chatter, vendors yelling, and music filling the air was like being in the heart of Hong Kong or Beijing. And too, the thickness in the air from cars, shops, and smokers seemed like being at home – in China.

In spite of the pushing, shoving and jostling of people to get a taxi, Kim's family managed to thrust themselves, without notice, in line and some how dart into the first cab that was not occupied.

Although the hotel was only 4 miles away, the streets were so jammed packed with people, buses, cars and taxies that it took more than 30 minutes to get to the Days Inn at the corner of 48th Street and 8th Avenue.

When the family was finally taken to their rooms on the 9th floor, everyone was relieved to unload their bags and relax, except for one problem. The stench was unbearable. "Oh no! This is a smoker's room; we requested non-smoker," Kim's mother noticed immediately. So, before Kim could take a break in the action, he went to a small tobacco shop across the street from the hotel and bought a cheap Bic lighter and a small pack of incense. After returning to the room, he lit the incense in each room to cover the rooms' thick smell of smoke; then, he stuck the lighter into his backpack. Unfortunately, the atmosphere in the rooms would not allow Kim and his family to take a nap; so, they decided to go out for dinner and take a walk afterwards to familiarize themselves with the area. They hoped the rooms' smell would diminish while they were gone and they could return to enjoy the comfort of the suite.

The next morning, Kim and his family woke early and prepared for a full day of sightseeing. After breakfast, they rushed out of the hotel to catch a taxi to "Ground Zero."

Standing at "Ground Zero" was an unbelievable sight. Of course, the entire area was fenced off to protect the public from injuries; but, the size of the area was far greater than Kim or his family members could have imagined. The television, magazines and newspapers' pictures could not capture the reality of the actual size, or the depth of the holes in the ground. People were taking pictures of the site, taking pictures of pictures of the Twin Towers, and taking pictures of the tourists' reactions to seeing the destruction caused by evil.

The ferry to Liberty Island was a short walk from "Ground Zero," so Kim and his family headed toward the statue of Liberty. Liberty Island, like "Ground Zero," was crowded with tourists and the statue of Liberty loomed into the bright blue sky. After touring the island and taking a few pictures, the family decided to have lunch in Chinatown; thus, - hungry and exhausted - back to the ferry and Battery Park they went.

Squeezed into a tiny area of lower Manhattan, New York's Chinatown, the second largest Chinatown in the United States, has remained an immigrant enclave and retains its unique cultural personality. Businesses and people pour out of storefronts and onto the sidewalks where the art of bargaining is always a challenge. In some cases, the narrow streets force the crowds of people to compete with moving vehicles for space. But none of this seemed a problem to Kim and his family; "Shenma chi fan?" What to eat was the big question at the moment. For, their focus centered on deciding which of the more than 300 restaurants in Chinatown would get their business. Kim wanted Peking duck; his parents wanted noodles, and his grandparents preferred dumplings or seafood. Fresh fish and steamed vegetables got the deciding vote.

Just as Kim's grandparents entered the door of a nearby seafood restaurant, the lights went out. At first, no one thought much about it; everyone, Kim, his parents, grandparents, restaurant owner, employees and customers all believed it to be a temporary power failure. With time to kill, Kim decided to go to the restrooms and wash before dinner, thinking – of course – the power would be restored by the time he returned to the table.

Even though there was still enough light to read the menu, everyone decided to wait. And wait they did. As the wait got longer, the mood in the dinning area changed from surprise, to funny, to curious, to worry. Finally, a few patrons decided to leave. Kim's father was the first to suggest leaving the restaurant, "We need to leave this place before we roast to death." With no lights and no air conditioning, the restaurant quickly lost its reputation as a safe heaven from the scourging heat outside. Therefore, Kim and his family decided to take a cab and eat back at the hotel.

As soon as Kim and his family left the restaurant, they quickly learned the streets were more crowded than before. It seemed as though the power failure was throughout Chinatown, and all the shops were emptying as customers, employees and owners were loitering around waiting for electricity and air conditioning.

In a very short time, the streets rapidly became a river of people flowing in one direction. Office buildings began to empty; storefronts, shops and subways were now contributing to the mass of people that now crammed the streets. It was now obvious this was no longer a temporary power failure. Kim and his family soon learned the entire city's electricity was out.

As Kim and his family headed toward Broadway to catch a taxi uptown, the throng of people grew. Waving a taxi had become impossible; taxies, buses, trucks, vans, cars and even motorcycles were all jam-packed and over capacity. The only people not moving were the street vendors selling bottled water to heat exhausted individuals.

For Kim's grandparents, to walk more than 50 New York City blocks would prove to be unbearable, especially on an empty stomach and in tormenting heat.

Kim noticed two empty yellow cabs parked in front of a small outdoor market. "Mom, Dad, stand at the side of these taxies; hold onto the door handles if you must, while I search for the drivers," Kim told his parents. It was his thought that maybe the drivers were in the market taking a lunch break. Therefore, if they waited long enough, one of the taxis would be available to get them back to the hotel. More than an hour passed and neither driver returned to their taxi. But, just as the family decided to continue their journey - on foot -to the hotel, a taxi came out of no where and the driver asked Kim's grandparents if they needed a cab. What luck!

It was 8 O'clock in the evening when Kim and his family arrived at the hotel. Some people were sitting in the dark lobby, but most had made themselves comfortable sitting outside on the curb or leaned against the hotel wall, while crowds of people continued to flow pass.

Kim and his family squeezed themselves in a small space on the curb. After an hour, Kim's mother relented, as she considered her parents health, "We can't stay here all night." "Then we'll stay close together, take out time, hold hands and make our way back to our rooms," Kim's father offered. Everyone, knowing it was going to be a challenge, but felt there was no other option, agreed.

Kim remembered he had the cigarette lighter in his backpack. Taking it out, he volunteered to lead the way to the 9th floor, lighting the dark stairways with the lighter. Holding on to each other's shirttail, and staying close to the walls, the family made their way, very slowly, to the 9th floor. As they climbed the stairs, step-by-step, Kim yelled out the number of steps to reach each landing. Kim was able to give his thumb – from time-to-time – a very short rest from the lighter because the hotel had strategically placed flashlights on various floors throughout the stairways.

Once the family reached the 9th floor, after climbing 18 flights of stairs, they exited the stairway into the hotel hall. It was pitch black and the red light from the exit sign over the stairway door did nothing to break through the thick blackness of the hallway. All that could be heard coming from the darkness was talking, yelling and laughter.

Before the family proceeded into the black corridor, Kim and his father had to determine which direction they would travel. Also, finding their rooms called for realizing they were approaching their rooms from the opposite direction of the elevator. Therefore, everything they knew about the 9th floor was now backwards, that is, left was right. And too, the 8th room from the elevator may now be 12. The only positive or sure thing they could count on was the key fitting the door.

Because Kim had the lighter, he gave instructions, "Stay close to the wall so as to not step on anyone and to keep your balance." Like moles traveling through a dark hole, the family ventured off into the blackness. When the exhausted group finally reached their rooms and opened the door, the cool air that was trapped in the room, left from the air conditioner, felt great, even though it did not last long.

Kim's grandparents and parents entered the rooms first. Just as he was about to turn and follow his father into the room, Kim heard moaning in the darkness. Kim went to investigate.

As Kim followed the yowling sounds of a woman, the screaming and screeching got louder and louder. When Kim reached the door of the crying and weeping sounds, his lighter illustrated a Philippine woman pouched on the floor; he immediately ran to her. "Oh my God!" she's pregnant.

Without hesitation, Kim instantly retrieved blankets and pillows from the bed to make her comfortable, and gave her a large glass of water to quench her thirst. Then, "Just relax; stay calm and I'll be back with help as soon as I can," as he dashed for the blacken stairways, leaving his Bic lighter with the lady.

Going down the stairs was much easier than the climb up; after all, he had counted each step, the hotel had put flashlights on various stairs, and he knew how many stairs there were between the 9th and 1st floor.

After warning the desk clerk of the emergency on the 9th floor, Kim scurried back through the darken stair tunnels anxious to get back to the pregnant lady.

Finding her room was much easier the second time. When Kim arrived at the lady's door, he was just seconds behind her husband and 15 year old son; "Don't worry; I've already warned the front desk of the problem and help should be here soon," Kim informed them. There in the darkness, as they waited for the ambulance, with Kim's Bic lighter providing occasional shadows dancing on the walls, the four of them bonded their relationship with tales of the New York City Black Out.

The power was still off the next morning as Kim and his family members prepared to return home.

The lobby of the hotel and the streets outside were bulging with people; but, because it was Saturday morning, getting a taxi to the train station wasn't as difficult as the previous day. However, the train station was jammed with people trying to leave the city. People were everywhere, and the air was thick with chatter and the smell of sweat.

Kim's grandparents and mother found space at the top of the stairs leading down into the train station. There they could at least catch a breeze, from time-to-time, as the wind would rush in the station. In the meantime, Kim and his father waited in long slow moving lines to get tickets. Nevertheless, they were successful in getting tickets for a 2 O'clock departure, and when they returned to the family's camp site, cold juice was waiting for them – courtesy of the American Red Cross.

The only thing left for the family to do was to sit in the shade, capture a cool breeze whenever possible, watch the throngs of people scampering about, and wait for 2 O'clock.

The trip to New York City proved to be more than just another weekend vacation, but rather a 24-hour adventure.

Lost Peony

On a bright and sunny day on the great grassy plains of Outer Mongolia, near the Chinese border, a small band of Mongolian nomads were preparing for the winter months. The women were unpacking and unrolling assorted animal hide to be used for their circular huts. The men were busy preparing the wooden frames to which the hides were to be attached. The children too had their roles to play. Some, the smaller children, cared for the livestock. They made sure the animals were safe, locked in, and fed. The older children helped the adults. Boys, of course, helped the men, and the girls helped the women. Finally, the elders either supervised or started preparing the evening meal, and either the men or women assumed these tasks.

For the casual observer, the tribe may seem to be clumsy and in discord, but nothing could be further from the truth. These nomads have performed their tasks so many times, that they can be fully established by dinner.

But this day was no ordinary day. For on this day, vibrations coming from the earth were startling the animals, and the little children were having a difficult time managing the larger animals.

The reason for the animals' nervousness would soon be discovered when the roar of an engine filled the air. All of the adults in the tribe stopped, turned in the direction of the sound, and then slowly started toward the noise. The children, frozen in their spots, could not understand what was happening. However, Gao Zhen Bi, a 10-year-old girl, took shelter behind a small grassy swelling protected by a few large rocks. It soon became apparent to all the children, even Gao Zhen Bi, that the strange noise was nothing to fear. As the sound grew louder and the adults' shouts could be heard, *qi che,* the arrival of a car was obvious. Even though many of the children had never seen a car before, that did not stop most of them from joining in the excitement and ran toward the adults, except Gao Zhen Bi. She stayed hidden.

For Gao Zhen Bi, this was not unusual behavior. She always seemed to be the last person to join any sort of celebration, activity or attraction. Even though she was smart, bright, quick to learn, and loved by everyone, Gao Zhen Bi never felt comfortable being *baoqui,* valuable or precious. In fact, rather than wear her status as a badge of honor, Gao Zhen Bi shunned any attention, except when she rode a horse. Only then, as she raced across the grassy fields did Gao Zhen Bi feel connected with this world.

"I can't believe I'm here," Kim thought to himself. "After so many years of dreaming of coming

14

to the wilderness, experiencing the lives of the nomads, getting to know them and their ways; Wow! It's really happening," Kim continued to muse. When the jeep finally stopped, within seconds, a small crowd surrounded the occupants as they emerged. Mary McHenry-Robinson, an anthropologist, was the first to get out of the jeep. She was an elderly Caucasian woman with a full head of white hair; she wore glasses and she was dressed in heavy winter-like clothing: boots, scarf, jacket, sweater and gloves. The nomads found this funny. For the tribe, it hadn't begun to get cold. They were still dressed in warm, but single layered, clothing. When the driver emerged from the jeep, he too was dressed in winter-like clothes. But few people paid him any attention. The driver, you see, was an Asian, i.e., Yee Kim Poy. In fact, he was more than a driver; he was Ms. Robinson's interpreter and a lawyer who was on a three month sabbatical from a prestigious law firm in America.

As the chatter and excitement filled the air, Gao Zhen Bi, peeping from her hideaway, felt more relaxed and decided to come out of hiding. Her decision to join the others was not only out of her curiosity for Ms. Robinson, but also because the driver (Yee Kim Poy) looked very much like her *lao shi,* teacher.

As Gao Zhen Bi slowly rose from the earth, Ms. Robinson, who was trying to be respectful to the elders and leaders, was also inspecting the tribe for personal reasons. And when Ms. Robinson saw Gao Zhen Bi off in the distance, dressed in a solid red outfit and knee high boots, her long blond single braid flapping in the wind, and her pale skin reflecting the sun's rays like a mirror, Ms. Robinson's feelings soared. For Ms. Robinson, seeing Gao Zhen Bi was like finding a rare flower, a lost peony, in the most unlikely of places. In her heart, Ms. Robinson felt as though she had just won an enormous lottery.

For the past 30 years, Ms. Robinson's research project has focused on trying to prove the existence of a lost female warrior tribe. Her most recent discovery, in Southern Russia, was the skeletal remains of a female warrior. The burial site and its contents also suggested that the female warrior, was not only a member of a large group, but this particular female was probably a high priest, the leader, or the Empress. Ms. Robinson was attempting to learn what happened to the tribe. It was her thought that the female warriors were defeated and taken as captives. As prisoners, the female warriors migrated with their captors and married their conquerors. However, many of the female warriors are believed to have escaped and started a new life in a new country. It is Ms. Robinson's guess that the new tribe and country was the nomads of Outer Mongolia. But, Ms. Robinson had no proof of her theory. Still, the possibility existed that she could prove her theory right, if she could find an individual with the same DNA as the skeletal remains of the female warrior she found in Southern Russia. And for Ms. Robinson, Gao Zhen Bi was her last hope, and if she were related to the Empress, 2500 years of DNA would have been transmitted to Gao Zhen Bi.

For now, Ms. Robinson's attention had to shift from Gao Zhen Bi to the tribe's elders. Ms. Robinson's challenge was to convince the nomad leaders that she meant no harm to their *baogui,* and taking her DNA would not diminish her value or appearance.

After living with the nomads for several weeks, Ms. Robinson learned their customs, ceremonies and rituals. One of the tribe's favorite rituals was to sit around the evening fire, with the elders, and tell tales about the tribe's history. Some of the stories were funny; some of the stories were full of danger, and still others were acts of heroism. Ms. Robinson's opportunity to reveal her real intent for visiting the tribe came one night when she was asked to tell a story about her history. Ms. Robinson, through her interpreter - Kim - told the story of the Amazon female warriors and the skeleton she found in Russia.

Realizing she had captured the tribes' imagination with her story, Ms. Robinson took a big risk by telling the tribe that she thought Gao Zhen Bi was a relative of the Empress. This idea that Gao Zhen Bi had royal blood in her veins was startling and confusing to the members. They knew Gao Zhen Bi was different, with her blond hair, hazel eyes and pale skin, but was her difference a result of her royal blood or had the gods, as they all believed, touched her? The question Ms. Robinson needed answered was, "Would the elders allow her to compare Gao Zhen Bi's DNA with the Empress'?"

Three days later, Ms. Robinson got her answer. The elders had decided to allow Ms. Robinson to make the DNA comparison. One of the reasons for the elders' decision was based on the fact that they and Gao Zhen Bi could not lose; that is, the gods blessed her or she was directly related to the ancient Empress, either way Gao Zhen Bi was still *baoqui* – precious.

Ten days after the DNA sample was sent off to Germany, the answer arrived in the small Mongolian village. Of course, the entire tribe was excited about Gao Zhen Bi's lineage. So, that evening, after dinner, the group gathered around the evening fire to tell stories that were more exciting and mysterious than the earlier stories. This night, like the earlier night, Ms. Robinson's story telling time came last. For Ms. Robinson, this night was far different than her first story of the ancient female warriors. This story telling session meant she would offer another explanation for Gao Zhen Bi's difference, or confirm the elders' belief about her exceptional beauty.

Ms. Robinson, with Kim's help, retold her earlier story about the Amazon female warriors, adding a few more details not told before. As she told the story, the stillness of the night and the heart beats of the group could be heard over the wild calls of the animals that roamed the nights. Just as Ms. Robinson told the group that Gao Zhen Bi's DNA and those of the skeletal remains of the Empress were a perfect match, the cracking wood of the fire sent a bust of red ambers shooting into the air, and the flash of energy from the blast lit up Gao Zhen Bi's face like a full moon against a black sky.

The next morning as Ms. Robinson and Kim were preparing to leave, they saw Gao Zhen Bi, in her red outfit and knee high boots, riding along the horizon, almost motionless atop the horse, with only her long blond braid trailing her profile. Kim couldn't help but to think of how many times the Empress must have performed the same dance.

LUCKY

Yee Kim Poy was born in Tai Yuan, Shan Xi, the People's Republic of China (PRC) in the year of the rabbit and he was affectionately called *Xiao Tu* (Little Rabbit) by his parents; he was an only child. Yu Xiao Hong was born 6 months later. Years later, her English speaking friends would call her April and Xiao Tu would call her *Meimei* (Little sister). She too was an only child and their parents had been friends for years; in fact, they all lived in the same apartment building. Because of the parents' relationship and because Xiao Tu and Meimei were so close, they were raised like brother and sister.

When Xiao Tu was 7 years old, he was a typical youngster who loved to play ball, play games, developed an interest in sports, always had a new best friend, and showed no interest in girls. Meimei, his little sister, was the exception; he enjoyed her company but only if there were no boys to play with. Still, Xiao Tu was very protective of Meimei; he would not allow other boys to tease or treat her mean. Meimei, on the other hand, was a very serious girl for her age. A little shy, but not so much that others would ignore her; her presence was always felt. She was a beautiful little girl who enjoyed being with Xiao Tu; they played together very well and she enjoyed the special attention she received when it was just the two of them. "Meimei, come read with me; my auntie Lu sent me another book from America."

By the time Xiao Tu and Meimei reached their teens, their relationship took a dramatic twist, at least for Meimei. That is to say, as Xiao Tu got more and more interested in Tennis and his studies, he did not seem to have time or interest in girls. Whereas, Meimei, not really interested in boys, was definitely fantasizing a romance with Xiao Tu. And even though he never expressed the same level of infatuation toward Meimei, she did not feel emotionally rejected by Xiao Tu; and because she knew he was not emotionally attached to another girl, she always felt she was his "girl-friend." In her mind, their "brother-sister" relationship was stronger than ever. "Xiao Tu, I need help at the market; do you think you could come with me?" Yu Xiao Hong asked in another attempt of making their relationship exclusive.

When they both attended Shan Xi University, nothing changed. They both looked forward to attending college together. For Xiao Tu, it was because he was embarking on a new adventure, i.e., challenging studies and the competition of being on the Tennis team. And too, he thought he could keep an eye on his little sister. But for Meimei, college was just another opportunity to protect and guard her personal interest in her "Tu Tu" from some college girl who might be looking for a husband.

From Xiao Tu's perspective, their college life was no different than it had always been. He continued to absorb himself into his studies and the competition of tennis. Whatever free time he had was spent with Meimei or a small group of friends. The only personal time Meimei got to spend with Xiao Tu was during Spring Festival when their families got together to celebrate. Still, Meimei's feelings for Xiao Tu never waived; In fact, the older they got the more she loved him. But she was too shy and too traditional to tell him. "One day it will be as it should be," she imaged.

Four years of college blew pass much too fast for Meimei; and, what added insult to injury was for her to learn that Xiao Tu was going to America for graduate school; she cried until her eyes were dry. She feared she was going to lose Xiao Tu to an American stranger. After all, she knew how permissive the American girls were, and she wasn't confident that her Tu Tu would remain or retain his innocence once he traveled abroad and was exposed to the trappings of lust and luxury. Nevertheless, Meimei made Xiao Tu promise to write regularly. "You mustn't break your promise," she insisted. Her intentions were to remain in his life and keep the two of them connected, and to reassure herself that he had not fallen in love with an American.

Xiao Tu went off to America, now calling himself Kim; and Meimei went to Beijing, where April became her adopted American name. She got a job with the Xinhua News Agency; there, April excelled as a daily news reporter. As for the letters between her and Kim, at first they were very regular; but after a year or so, Kim's letters became less and less, until they finally stopped. For April, her worst fears were tearing at her heart. Kim was lost in the abyss of Americanism.

Eventually the pain and the apparent lost faded away, and April buried herself in work. By the end of April's second year in Beijing, her parents began pressuring her to marry and start a family; after all, she wasn't getting any younger, and all the "good" young men would be gone. "You're not getting any younger, and we want a grand son," her mother wrote. April did start dating but only to keep her parents at bay; she wasn't serious nor was she thinking about marriage. Her parents, of course, were introducing her – at every chance they got – to all the "good" sons of their friends.

April wasn't sure if it was her parents, her own realization that her "clock" was ticking, or her tired will to keep the fight going, but she started steady dating a successful businessman – Wang Kun. Her office girl friends were excited and happy for her, and they too pressured her to accept a proposal of marriage. The pressure from all sides began to take their toll. April was entertaining thoughts; even though she hadn't felt for Wang Kun what she felt for Kim, she found qualities in Wang Kun she liked; and, the more she looked, the more she convinced herself she could be happy with him.

Kim, now graduated from Harvard Law School, decided to return home for a one month visit before starting to work for a prestigious law firm in Washington D.C.. He was desperate to see his family again; for him the last three years had been an eternity. Besides, he missed all of his boyhood friends and classmates, and his curiosity about his little sister gnawed at his conscious; he was embarrassed about the broken promise - the letters.

Kim spent the first three weeks in Tai Yuan. The home cooked meals, the visits with classmates and professors at Shan Xi University, and soccer games with boyhood friends were accelerating. But what he had not counted on was the many introductions his mother had arranged with all the "suitable" young ladies. "Be sure and look your best tonight; we're having guests for dinner," he was reminded by his mother. Kim's parents, like April's, thought it was time for him to marry and start his family. Like their good friends, they were eager for grandchildren. It was during these three weeks Kim learned that April was a successful reporter in Beijing, and she too might be getting married soon. This news stunned Kim; he could not imagine his Meimei being married; he also learned, to his amazement, he missed seeing his little sister. Thus, it was not a surprise to anyone when he announced he was going to Beijing to surprise April with a visit; besides, he wanted to get away from the too eager young ladies willing to marry a perfect stranger – him.

One of the first things Kim did once he was settled in Beijing was to buy April a present. He planned to surprise her at work and then take her out to lunch. When he arrived at the newspaper, he asked, "Yu Xiao Hong, Nali?" Kim discovered April was out to lunch at a nearby restaurant. The girls at the office were more than happy to help Kim locate April, especially when he introduced himself as her brother. Not only were they shocked and surprised to learn April had a brother, but when they learned he was educated in America, single and handsome, they all expected to see more of Kim by means of April.

Kim entered the restaurant looking for a young lady with a long braid down her back, dressed conservatively, and probably as thin as a rail. Scanning the room, he saw a couple in the corner; the lady, sitting near a large bamboo plant, had her back to him. Thinking he could sneak up on April, like he had done many times in the pass, he would scare and surprise her. After all, she had no idea he was even in China; this would be easy. Just as Kim was within a few feet of the couple, the young lady turned to look about the room. It was then that Kim discovered it wasn't April. How embarrassed he would have been. He felt relieved and a little confused because now he couldn't find April at all. He was sure he was in the correct restaurant. He scanned the room again. No April. So, he returned to her office to wait.

The buzz in the office was obvious; April's girl friends were eager to entertain Kim as he waited. Each young lady was vying for more attention than the other. He was offered tea; he was offered to share a lunch; he was offered to go to lunch, and he was offered, although discreetly, a date. He politely refused all offers. Although, the wait for April was not a total waste; Between conversations and offers, Kim got an opportunity to see how April lived; that is, in her cubical, there were old pictures of Kim and April when they were in college; there were pictures of their families' gatherings and pictures of them together before Kim went to America. The pictures not only reminded Kim of how much time had passed, but they also reminded him of how much he really missed his little sister.

"Zaijian," Wang Kun said at the front door of the newspaper building. "Goodbye," April responded, and they went their separate ways, planning, of course, to see each other later that evening.

As April entered the office, not only did she notice and feel a change in the air, but she could see her girl friends' expressions light up when they all saw her coming. And, the closer she got to them, the more she could see someone, with their back to her, sitting at her desk. This was definitely confusing. Everyone seemed to be busting with excitement, but April was too focused on the stranger in her chair to inquire about the apparent delight.

Simultaneously, as April entered the office, Kim turned in the swivel chair. Their eyes met instantly. For a split second, both were frozen; Kim with amazement and April with shocked. She wasn't sure if the person in front of her was Kim or not; after all, it had been three years and people change. Kim was frozen because the beauty in front of him was not the little sister he left behind. The young lady was dressed in the latest New York fashion; her hair was styled like one of the many models he saw on billboards in Boston. In fact, Kim thought the model in front of him was blocking his view of April; he attempted to look around her. But just as quickly as time stopped, they both rushed to embrace the other. "Xiao Tu!" … "Meimei!"

For the first time in his life, Kim felt inferior to his little sister. April was not only the mature lady he had always known, but now she was a successful reporter, a celebrity, a boss, and a stunning beauty.

April forgot about Wang Kun. Kim was back in her life; and just as always, she was in love – again. But this time, she had competition; her office girl friends and her best friend; she didn't know it yet, but the "cat fight" was about to begin. "Excuse us ladies, but can we have a moment?" she asked politely.

Learning Kim was only going to be in Beijing for a few days before returning to Tai Yuan and then to America, April decided to take time off from work and show Kim around Beijing. She also planned to return to Tai Yuan with Kim; this would allow her to spend more time with him; it would allow her to visit her parents, which she had put off for far too long, and it would allow their families to get together one more time before their worlds disappeared.

The week in Beijing with Kim was unbelievable. Kim and April took tours of the city, visited the Summer Palace, the Forbidden City, climbed the Great Wall, ate at the best restaurants, relaxed in the park, took in an opera, and – of course – shopped. For the most part, April and Kim were alone, but many times April's girl friends had invited themselves. Nevertheless, April enjoyed every moment of it; for once in their long history, she was in control of their relationship. But like everything else, the week went much too fast. Needless to say, Kim too enjoyed these outings, and for the first time he began looking at April with different eyes. "I'm amazed at how much you've changed; not only in your appearance – which is lovely – but how you take charge and lead your staff," he offered. "I have no choice; the job is very demanding," April responded, trying not to sound obnoxious.

The train ride to Tai Yuan would be at least 8 hours, and for Kim and April it would also be a rare opportunity, since he left for America, for the two of them would be alone – even if it was in a crowd. It would also be the first time Kim looked into the eyes of April and felt something different. That is, not like a big brother but rather a stranger meeting a beautiful lady for the first time. For Kim, the occasional and accidental touching between the two of them only added to his emotional struggle.

April's mother knew something was different with April long before the families' final dinner together. She didn't know what was behind April's elevated personality, but she sensed a major change in her daughter. To her, April had the exuberance of a 15 year old school girl, the playfulness of an 8 year old, and the cheeriness of a woman in love. April's mother thought it was because April was coming to terms with being married to Wang Kun. But, the truth would be discovered when both families were re-living an old tradition they had established years ago. When the children graduated from elementary school, there was a big family dinner. When the children graduated from high school, there was a big family dinner. When the children passed their college entrance examinations, there was a big family dinner. When the children graduated from college, there was a big family dinner. When Kim was accepted into Harvard Law School and April accepted a prestigious job with a national news agency in Beijing, there was a big family dinner. Now, Kim had accepted a position in Washington D.C. with a prominent law firm and April was marrying a successful businessman from Beijing; therefore, there was cause for a big family dinner. It would go without saying, both families were extremely proud of their children's success; all one would have to do is to ask a neighbor; they all knew.

At the family dinner, April's mother discovered it first. It wasn't the up-coming marriage that made her daughter seem so glib and poised. It was Kim's presence. April was in love with Kim. Did Kim's parents recognize this? Was Kim aware of this? What about Wang Kun? How could she marry one man and be in love with another?

Kim's parents, on the other hand, attributed the children's different behavior to "growing pains." Kim was more mature, better educated, and exposed to the American culture. Of course he would be a "little" different. Whereas, April, always a serious girl, was a celebrity in Beijing and was about to become the wife of a successful professional. So, aside from their occasional English conversations, which they would have in the presence of their parents to pass secrets, Kim's parents were oblivious to the potential drama.

Two days before Kim's departure, he and April had made plans to have one more private dinner together before they would fulfill their parents' dreams. Each knew their lives would not be the same - ever again. Kim would be off in America making a new life for himself, with only occasional visits home. April would be establishing a new life in Beijing, and the opportunity for such privacy between them would be all but impossible.

The dinner with April had gone well. She had picked the restaurant. It was the one very near Shan Xi University where they had went many times before. The menu never changed, but the food was better. And, the new owners had some remodeling completed. These small incidentals offered conversation and laughter as they verbally strolled down memory lane. Then, out of nowhere, Kim asked, "When did our roles reverse?"

"What are you talking about?" April answered with a puzzled look. "Usually men are the strong, confident ones; but with you, I feel mediocre. Like, I don't measure up." "That's silly; that doesn't make any sense, and you know it," April interjected, still trying to figure out what's on Kim's mind. With that, silence failed and the walk home seemed longer. Even though it was late, they decided to take the walk through the campus. And as they neared the small park behind the student ball room, Kim suggested they sit awhile. After all, he could sleep on the plane ride and April could rest up on the train back to Beijing.

Quietly they entered the small park; neither spoke as they approached the vine covered gazebo. As they sat, the bright moon bounced sparkles of light off April's face. Kim was hypnotized by her beauty. Then the silence was broken by the soft murmur of April's sobs, which she could not hold back.

Kim didn't know what to do. He had never witnessed April cry before (except for an injury like falling from her bike), and he had never found himself in the presence of a woman crying for no apparent reason. He was stunned; he felt helpless and confused. The only thing he could think of doing was to put his arms around April and ask, "What's the matter?" In his own mind, he thought it was the nervousness of the marriage. April, instead of revealing she had second thoughts about marrying Wang Kun, lashed out in anger at Kim's thoughtlessness. "How stupid you are!" Now he was definitely confused. She offered no explanation; she just sat quietly sobbing.

Kim, baffled by this sudden change of emotion, held her hand tenderly, still puzzled as to what to say or do. And as they sat in the stillness of the night air, his mind raced; he suddenly became aware that he was struggling to suppress disturbing thoughts. He started feeling guilty and ashamed of having amorous feelings for April. She was his little sister; wasn't she? He would be dishonoring their families by pursuing an incestuous love affair; wouldn't he?

Where do words come from? How does the mouth open and allow words out that have not been pre-approved? Doesn't the brain and mouth communicate before words are spoken? Kim didn't have the answers to these questions; all he knew was he had asked, "Do you want to go to America with me?" The words just shot out before he had a chance to scrutinize them. The words blasted out so fast, he found himself startled, but he couldn't take them back. It was the worst proposal ever made, but the toothpaste was out of the tube and it couldn't be put back.

In the millisecond between his last word – America – and April's response, Kim's heart froze with fear.

April's swift reaction was unexpected, but surprising clear. She lunged at him, throwing her arms around his neck, lifting herself from the ground, and squealed out … "YES!"

❝I loved reading your stories. The main personage Kim seems to be a not so fictional reminder of you. A very sweet story, filled with adventures, words of encouragement and hope told in a very upbeat manner which often brought a smile to my face. I will definitely recommend the book to the family and friends, and especially to the nieces and nephews. … Keep writing!"

—CA

Questions for Discussion

1. Why the title "Rainbow Seeker"?

2. In "Discoveries," what was the actual number of discoveries?

3. How did some of Kim's discoveries compare to some your own?

4. In the "Cruise," should Kim have gotten involved with the gang of boys; or, should he have minded his own business? Why?

5. Why do you think Kim was so quick to befriend the brother and sister in the "Cruise"?

6. What is behind Kim's desires to come to the rescue in both the "Cruise" and "The Black Out"?

7. How important was Kim's role in the "Lost Peony"?

8. Should he, or could he, have done more to help Dr. Robinson?

9. Who was the luckiest in "Lucky"? Why?

10. Who broke up the relationship or marriage between April and Wang Kun, April or Kim?

11. What is the main character trait that Kim demonstrates throughout all of the stories?

CPSIA information can be obtained
at www.ICGtesting.com
Printed in the USA
257239LV00002B

9781467038591